DATE

1-7-2020
8-14-2020
10-13-2020
4-20-2023

BRODART, CO.

BIZARRO ™

STONE ARCH BOOKS
a capstone imprint

AN ORIGIN STORY

DC Super-Villains Origins
are published by Stone Arch Books,
A Capstone Imprint
1710 Roe Crest Drive
North Mankato, Minnesota 56003
www.mycapstone.com

Cataloging-in-Publication Data is available on the Library of Congress website.
ISBN: 978-1-4965-7938-6 (library binding)
ISBN: 978-1-4965-8102-0 (paperback)
ISBN: 978-1-4965-7943-0 (eBook)

Summary: How did Bizarro become Superman's evil opposite? Discover the story behind this villain's journey from Man of Steel look-alike to backward baddie.

Contributing artists: Dario Brizuela
Designed by Hilary Wacholz

Printed in the United States of America.
102018 000048

BIZARRO

AN ORIGIN STORY

WRITTEN BY
IVAN COHEN

ILLUSTRATED BY
LUCIANO VECCHIO

SUPERMAN CREATED BY
JERRY SIEGEL AND JOE SHUSTER
BY SPECIAL ARRANGEMENT WITH
THE JERRY SIEGEL FAMILY

High in the mountains, a scientist works inside a small lab. He squirts drops of blood into a dish filled with chemicals. The chemicals quickly increase the number of blood cells in the dish.

"It's working!" the scientist tells his boss.

"Good," Lex Luthor says with a wicked smile.

The scientist places the cells into a liquid-filled tank. Soon the cells form the shape of a human. A creature has grown from Superman's blood!

"The experiment is nearly complete, Mr. Luthor," says the scientist.

"Not quite," replies Luthor.

He pulls a lever, and the tank opens. The liquid spills out onto the floor. Inside the empty tank, the creature takes its first breath.

A short time later, the strange being flies above downtown Metropolis. He feels like helping people in need.

FWOOSH!

Suddenly a red-and-blue figure streaks toward him. The creature comes face to face with his twin!

On the street below a girl cries out, "Look! Up in the sky . . . two Supermans!"

The creature studies the twin in front of him. "Who are you?" he asks.

"I am Superman," replies the real Man of Steel.

The creature becomes angry. "No you not! Me am Superman!" argues the twin. "Me show you!"

FWOOSH! The Superman twins soar toward the city below.

A few blocks away, an old building is on fire. Firefighters quickly arrive at the scene. They pull out hoses and blast flames with streams of water.

"Me stop building from getting wet!" cries the twin. He flies in front of the hoses to block the water.

"No!" shouts the real Man of Steel. The super hero tries to stop the strange being from hurting anybody.

"Me help more people!" shouts the Superman twin.

The creature spots a nearby bridge opening for a tall ship. "Me fix broken bridge!" he says.

Using his super-strength, the Superman twin presses the bridge back together.

"Stop!" shouts the real Man of Steel. The bridge is too low for the ship to pass through!

The real Superman soars toward the ship. The hero stops the ship before it can crash into the bridge.

People along the shore cheer for the Man of Steel.

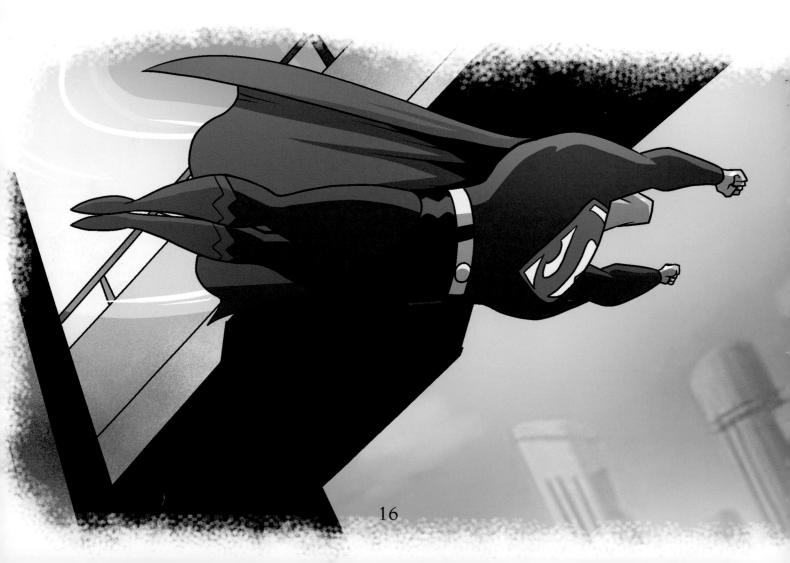

"They no like you," says the confused creature. "Me stop you!"

The Superman twin flies at the real Man of Steel with all his might.

SMAAASH! The titans battle each other in midair. The twin's powers are the exact opposite of Superman's.

Instead of freeze breath, the twin blasts flame breath. Instead of Superman's heat vision, the twin fires freeze vision!

The Superman twin is no match for the real Man of Steel. The strange being flees to Lex Luthor's mountainside lab.

When he arrives, the creature no longer looks super. His arms and legs are twisted. His skin is pale.

"Look at him!" cries the scientist. "He's no Superman. He's bizarre!"

"This Bizarro may have failed," says Luthor. "But one of these experiments will surely be a success!"

Luthor flicks a switch, revealing a dozen liquid-filled tanks. All the tanks contain Superman twins.

Luthor's true plan is finally revealed: he is building an entire army of Superman clones!

WHAM! The real Man of Steel crashes through the lab's ceiling.

"Superman!" shouts Luthor.

"He no Superman!" shouts Bizarro. "Me am Superman!"

Bizarro grows angry. The creature begins smashing the equipment around him. He strikes a button that will destroy the entire lab!

"He's your problem now!" Luthor shouts at Superman. The evil businessman and his scientist escape the lab. Superman soars after them.

Suddenly—*KA-BOOM!*—the lab explodes in a fiery blast!

Superman believes that Bizarro has been buried in the explosion.

Moments later, Bizarro crawls out of the rubble. He stands and looks out at the city of Metropolis below.

"Bizarro need new home," says the strange creature.

FWOOSH! Bizarro streaks toward the city.

At the same time, the real Man of Steel heads in the opposite direction!

SMAAASH!

Bizarro crashes into a Metropolis water tower with all his might. The tower starts to crack. Water sprays onto citizens below.

People scream and run.

"Why they scream?" asks Bizarro. "Me turn shiny city into pretty ruins!"

Superman returns wearing a special suit. The suit protects the super hero from the powerful weapon he carries: Kryptonite.

Kryptonite is Superman's greatest weakness. But it doesn't stop Bizarro!

"Glowing rock beautiful," says Bizarro, grabbing the radioactive rock. "Me thank Superman by ruining city more!"

Just then, Superman realizes that Bizarro isn't a super-villain. He just wants to be a hero but does everything backward.

"Wait!" shouts the Man of Steel.

Bizarro stops before more damage is done. "What Superman want?" asks Bizarro.

"Come with me," Superman tells the backward hero. "I know a planet that needs your help more than Earth!"

Superman and Bizarro soar into the far reaches of space. The Man of Steel leads the backward creature to a small, empty planet.

"This world needs protecting," Superman says. "I call it Bizarro World."

Bizarro frowns.

"Don't you like it?" asks the Man of Steel.

"This am happy frown," the backward twin replies.

Even with a new home, Bizarro often returns to Earth. When he does, Bizarro's backward powers are a danger to the people of Metropolis.

The strange creature is often Superman's enemy.

But sometimes he is the exact opposite—a true friend.

EVERYTHING ABOUT . . .

BIZARRO ™

REAL NAME: UNKNOWN

CRIMINAL NAME: BIZARRO

ROLE: SUPER-VILLAIN

BASE: MOBILE

Bizarro is a botched clone of Superman. This doppelganger's superpowers are the exact opposite of Superman's. While he tries to be just like the Man of Steel, he never quite gets it right and ends up causing trouble instead.

THE AUTHOR

IVAN COHEN is a former editor and media-development executive at DC Comics. As a writer, Cohen's recent credits include the *Green Lantern: The Animated Series* comic book, articles for *Time Out* magazine, and an episode of the Cartoon Network television series *Beware the Batman*. The co-producer of *Secret Origin: The Story of DC Comics*, Ivan was also a consultant on the PBS documentary *Superheroes: The Never-Ending Battle*.

THE ILLUSTRATOR

LUCIANO VECCHIO currently lives in Buenos Aires, Argentina. With experience in illustration, animation, and comics, his works have been published in the US, Spain, UK, France, and Argentina. His credits include Ben 10 (DC Comics), Cruel Thing (Norma), Unseen Tribe (Zuda Comics), Sentinels (Drumfish Productions), and several DC Super Heroes books for Capstone.

GLOSSARY

bizarre (bih-ZAHR)—unusual or odd

citizen (SIT-uh-zen)—a person who lives in a city or town

destroy (dih-STROY)—puts an end to something

lab (LAHB)—a place for making scientific experiments and tests

pale (PAYL)—light in color or shade

rubble (RUHB-uhl)—piles of rough or broken things

ruins (ROO-ihns)—the remains of something destroyed

titan (TYT-en)—someone of gigantic size and power

villain (VIL-uhn)—a wicked person

DISCUSSION QUESTIONS

Write down your answers. Refer back to the story for help.

QUESTION 1.

Do you think Bizarro is good, evil, or both? Explain your answer using examples from the story.

QUESTION 2.

Why do you think Superman found Bizarro a new planet to live on instead of destroying the super-villain?

QUESTION 3.

If you had an opposite twin, what would he or she be like? What would their name be? Discuss.

QUESTION 4.

What is your favorite illustration in this book? Explain how you made your decision.

READ THEM ALL!!

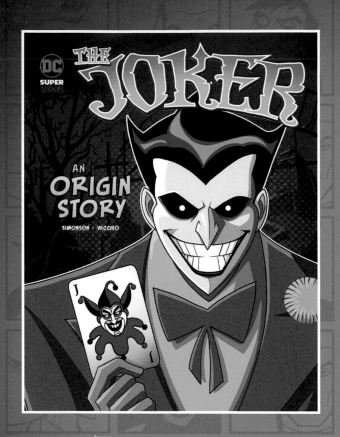

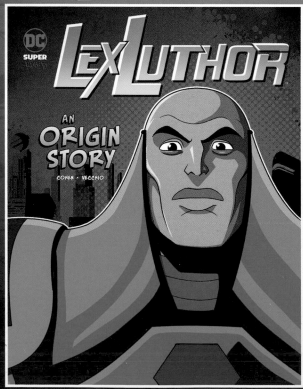